ROAD TO TRIUMPH

HARSHINI MAHESH

Contents

In a quiet corner of the bustling city, amidst the clamor of daily life, lived a small boy named "Dhruv", , and parents used to call him Tommy with Love he was just Fifteen years old, his eyes held with untold stories and a heart that weathered more than its fair share of storms!!! Orphaned at a young age, David world had been confined to the dimly lit corners.

FEW YEARS AGO : Dhruv who was young lived with his loving parents, There small home was filled with warmth and laughter. One fateful evening, a fierce storm rolled in, bringing with torrential rain and howling winds.

The storm causing the widespread flooding. The rivers overflowed and the streets submerged under rising waters.

Dhruv Parents ensured Dhruv's safety, they instructed him to stay in the attic, where they thought he would be safest. By the time emergency services reached the place , his parents had already been lost to the flood's relentless force!!

Then emergency services took him to orphanage!!
As the days passed one fine afternoon sun cast a golden glow over the orphanage, Dhruv was sitting by the window with a book in his lap.

The front door creaked open, and walked Grandma, a figure of gentle strength and unwavering kindness, holding a large suitcase. His eyes widened and hope danced across his face. Grandma smiled and with soft comforting voice, she called out, "Dhruv , My dear!!" her arms, open wide and hugged him tightly.
Dhruv, now feeling a deep sense of belonging , smiled up at her.

He could sense the new chapter beginning with her arrival and grandma took him to her place. Grandma been a source of strength and wisdom. She felt his loss in the very small age and boosted him to be stronger in his life.

Financial problems hit them very badly, grandma alone was looking after Everything .

Every morning , before the first light of dawn broke over the horizon, Grandma would lace up her boots and prepare for the long trek ahead .

She was determined to do whatever it look to support Dhruv and keep their small household running.

After her miles of walk and work in farm she used to get the vegetables from her own farm and filling the stomach of Dhruv. As the days passed energetic woman who walked miles each day for agriculture work began to show signs of weariness. Her steps, once firm and determined , became slower.

One Crisp evening ,Dhruv sat beside Grandma bed, "Dhruv" she said softly , her voice weak but filed with urgency.

"There's something I need to tell you". Dhruv leaned in closer , holding her hand gently.

"What is it Grandma?" Grandma told : Look my dear "All those years, the money I earned from the fields ....I saved it for you . It's buried in the garden, beneath the old oak tree." Dhruv's eyes widened in surprise.

And then Grandma replied "I wanted to make sure you had something to start with, something you build a better future by studying well and becoming the great successful person in the life " .

Promise me you'll use it wisely. Tears welled up in Dhruv's eyes as he nodded overwhelmed by her sacrifice. "I promise , Grandma ."

Dhruv sat by Grandma bedside, his hands gently clasping hers . Her breaths were shallow , and her face serene as if she were already dreaming of the peaceful rest that awaited her .The face told the story of a life filled with struggle, love and unwavering determination. As the first rays of morning light filtered through the curtains, Grandma *took one final, deep breath. Tears streamed down Dhruv's cheeks, as he screamed louder ....*

"Grandma , Please don't leave me alone" come back !!!. His heart ached with big loss.

The Next morning , he made his way to the garden , shovel in hand.

The oak tree stood tall and majestic , it's branches reaching out like protective arms over the garden , where grandma had spent so many hours . Dhruv sat under the tree for some time , with his heart filled with Big loss of all his persons in his life.

And the small boy was thinking how to live his life further ......

Dhruv begin to dig , the earthy smell of soil filling the air!! .

After several minutes of digging , the shovel struck something solid.

His heart raced as he unearthed a small wooden box. He opened it to reveal many coins and notes, carefully wrapped in cloth to protect them from the elements .The sight of the money brought a mix of emotions — Relief , gratitude and a deep sense of responsibility .

Grandma savings was a final gift to ensure Dhruv's future was secure.

As Dhruvstood by the Oak tree , holding the box of money . He felt the weight of his Grandma's legacy .

Grandma savings were more than a money — They were a symbol of her enduring love and the hope she had for Dhruv's future . As he looked out over the garden , Dhruv knew that her spirit was always be with him, guiding him as he embarked on his new chapter of his life .

CHAPTER TWO

PRESENT DAY :- *Dhruv with a small backpack and box of small money sat near the street ,his eyes held with untold stories and a heart that weathered more than its fair share of stormsand , who was Orphan*
.

And in the mind somewhere he still had a laziness of doing work and studying, The sadness was he don't wanted to Study.

By closing eyes he felt the words of his Grandma . Which she used to tell him everyday , " Look son ,you are very intelligent and talented you are just lazy to do everything , kick it out from your mind , if you think really you can do that , you will do it !!!

Just keep that luziness aside and start working on the things .

If you think "I have much time to do" or "I will start doing it tomorrow " It will never happen .
Don't listen to your mind , Listen to your heart what it tells . Just close your eyes take a deep breath and do it , It will show you the correct path of the life .

After remembering all these words told by his Grandma in past, He started his journey . He didn't have a specific destination in mind ; he wanted to escape the shadow of laziness .

He wandered from town to town .....as he traveled from town to town his thoughts often drifted to past .
His parents faces appeared in his eyes with startling clarity .

He remembered the Sound of his Mother's laughter , a melodic and joyful noise of his house , Motivational words of his grandma .

But he was trying a lot to come out of it .

He saw the children's of his age enjoying their life , who had everything which was satisfying them , Dhruv felt that even he wanted his life to build up like that and started thinking of what to do ?

After spending months on the Road , Dhruv decided it was time to establish a more stable routine.
He realized that to truly move forward and build a better future , he needed to return to education and find steady source of income .

With this , he sought out a local government school .

Enrolling in the Government school was hopeful step .

Dhruv was nervous and worried about fitting in with students , who were younger and had been in school continuously . The first few days at school were challenging as Dhruv adjusted to the academic environment and reconnected with discipline of studying.

He found himself struggling with some of the coursework but was committed to catching up.
His past experience had taught him the value of Hardwork and he approached his studies with perseverance .

Dhruv's teachers noticed his dedication and willingness to learn . They offered him encouragement and extra help , which he gratefully accepted .

Over time , he began to gain confidence in his academic abilities and completed his schooling and entered the Govt. PU college . To support

himself financially , Dhruv also took on a part – time job at a local café
.

The job involved serving customers , preparing orders , and handling various tasks around the café .
The work was physically demanding and required him to be on his feet for long hours , but Dhruv approached it with positive attitude .

The money he used to earn from his job he used to save same like his Grandma did , often he used to go near the Old oak tree , which was near his grandma home , he buried the money under the Tree and making it as a savings for his future .He didn't had a idea of savings amount in Bank so he used to follow his Grandma's secret plan.

Dhruv often found himself haunted by memories of his parents and Grandma. One evening , after a particularly long day of college and work , Dhruv returned to his small room , Exhausted. He placed his backpack on the floor and sat on the bed with mind full of feelings and stress.

The room was silent . As he stared out at the darkening sky , memories began to flood his mind . He remembered his mother laughter , a sound that filled their home with joy .
He recalled his Fathers strong reassuring presence .

The tears came suddenly , unexpected but not unwelcome. By holding the photo of his family , he traced their faces with his fingertips. The memories were bittersweet , a mix of love and loss that tugged at his heartstrings.
As usual he used to go to college one fine day , Some of his classmates , unable to understand or appreciate the value of hard work and responsibility , began to tease him for his job at the café .
They would make snide comments and laugh behind his back , calling him names like "Waiter boy" and "Coffee kid" .

Dhruv felt embarrassed and frustrated . He knew he was working at the café to support himself and save for his future , yet he was controlling all his frustration and minding his work .

One day , during lunch a particularly vocal bully made a derogatory comment about Dhruv's job . Instead of getting upset ,Dhruv smiled and said "YES , I work at a Café . Its great place , and I've learned a lot. Plus , I'm saving up for college . What about you?" His calm and confident response left the bully speechless and made others in the group reconsider their own attitudes. The situation took a darker turn when the bully , feeling insulted and resentful , decided to retaliate by targeting Dhruv's Savings.

One Evening Dhruv was walking towards the old oak tree near the Grandma home which was far away from rest of the houses , He was carefully keeping his money under the tree without knowing anyone , Bully and his friend followed him that evening and noticed all his secret savings.

Next day after the school Dhruv rushed to Job and Bully went near the old oak tree with few gang and took out all his savings .

Next day after the school Dhruv rushed to Job and Bully went near the old oak tree with few gang and took out all his savings .

Next day When Dhruv came to school , Bully sat behind him and started taunting "Hey , Dhruv " Bully sneered
"How's your oak tree doing ?is your money safe now ?"

Dhruv felt a surge and frustration . The bully's reference to the oak tree was a cruel reminder of where he used to hide his savings ,
He got tears in his eyes and He requested Bully to give back the money But Bully was a Cruel person and he didn't understand his feelings.

He told Dhruv to Apologize ' him in front of everyone where Dhruv insulted him during lunch break few days ago , And then with lot of calmness Dhruv replied please Give back my Money "I worked very hard for it , you have a happy family and I don't even have a family ....

I'm saving it for my bettercollege . Bully replied with Attitude ....Fine do one thing " Anyways you are interested in doing job !!

During lunch break polish my shoe in front of everyone and take back your money Bully replied ....Dhruv agreed and next day Afternoon Dhruv went near Bully and said "You think you're so smart and insulting me to do this in front of everyone? Dhruv's patience snapped.

The constant harassment , the robbery , and the endless taunts had pushed him to his limit . Without thinking , he swung his fist and punched the bully squarely in the face .

The bully staggered back , shocked and momentarily stunned by the force of Dhruv's blow .
The cronies looked on in surprise , unsure of how to react .

Dhruv breathing heavily , stood his ground , fists clenched and eyes blazing with anger.
"you've taken enough from me , "Dhruv shouted . "I'm done letting you push me around !" After listening to the loud shout all the staff came out and Mr. Harris , his mentor arrived the scene in a state of agitation. Acting on the assumption that Dhruv had initiated the violence without understanding the full context , Mr. Harris slapped Dhruv across the face .

Dhruv was stuned . The slap was not just a Physical shock but a profound emotional blow.

It felt like an injustice compound by the lack of understanding of his situation.

Dhruv's eyes welled with tears as he tried to process what had just happened.

"Sir , please , let me explain !" Dhruv protested , his voice shaking with a mix of anger and distress . "It's not what it looks like . I didn't start this."

Mr. Harris ,still visibly upset, paused and looked at Dhruv , "I didn't expect this from you , I thought you are very good student and I thought you are so responsible in your work at this small age , but you are not to my expectations" replied Mr. Harris.

At that moment Inishka ,Dhruv's classmate stepped forward , and voice spoke up .

"Sir please listen. Dhruv was provoked . He was being relentlessly bullied and pushed to his breaking point. He tried to handle it without violence , but it became too much."

Mr.Harris took a deep breath, realizing the gravity of the situation . He had acted out of frustration and desire to address the immediate issue of the fight, "I m sorry , Dhruv , " Mr. Harris said , his tone softening. And then they took action on Bully .

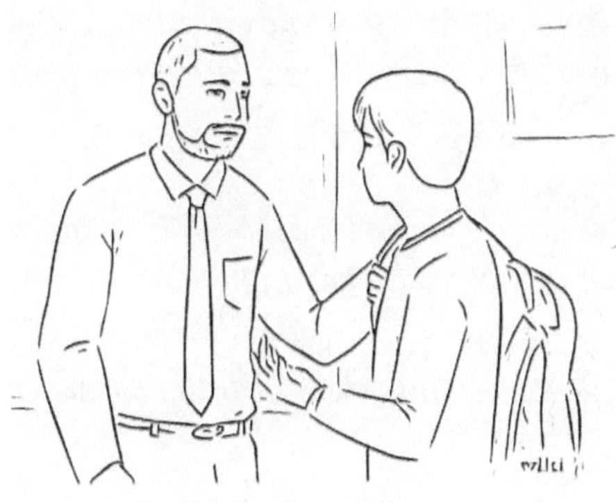

Then Dhruv thanked Inishka for coming forward , and then Inishka suggested him to meet the accountant who was well known to Inishka , they will help you out in Saving amount . Dhruv was happy for that and thanked her.

Inishka became his closest friend and started sharing few things .

He Found some group of friends , After enduring numerous hardships and challenges ,Dhruv poured his heart and soul into his studies .

The support from his friends and the lessons from his grandma , fueled his determination to succeed academically .

As the Final exams approached ,Dhruv spent countless hours preparing.

He balanced his part –time job at the café with his studies , often staying up late into the night to review his notes . When the final exams finally arrived.

Dhruv felt a wave of nervous excitement . He entered the examination hall with a determined mindset , ready to give his best effort .

After the exams were over , there was anxious wait for the results . when the results were out as the page loaded, his eyes scanned the screen , and wide smile spread across his face .

"He had done It"!! - Dhruv had achieved excellent marks in is final exams . He was not much excited and he didn't know with whom to share his happiness , he went towards the old oak tree and slept under the tree for some time , by filling the tears in his eyes and heart filled with lot of emotions.

CHAPTER THREE

Stepping onto the university campus for the first time, Dhruv felt both excited and anxious.

He was ready for this new chapter but knew it would be different from high school.

During the orientation week, Dhruv participated in various activities designed to help new students connect.

Rishi shared his passion for painting and his dream of one day hosting his own art exhibitions. Dhruv admired his creativity and the way he viewed the world through an artistic lens.

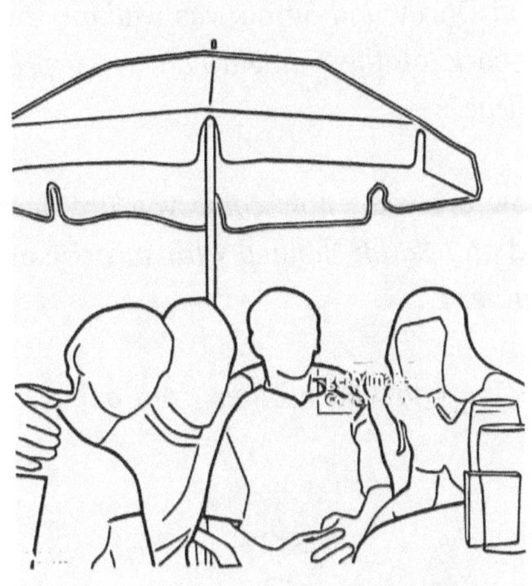

Rishi often invited Dhruv to art shows and encouraged him to explore his creative side, even if it was just through simple doodles during study breaks.

Viraj and Dhruv bonded over their shared interest in technology and innovation.

Viraj's analytical mind and Dhruv's business acumen led to many late-night discussions about potential startup ideas.

They even collaborated on a few small projects, combining their skills to create prototypes that they hoped to develop further in the future.

Sarah's kindness and empathy made her a natural confidante. She often organized study groups and was always ready to lend a listening ear when someone needed to talk.

Her dedication to her studies and her dream of becoming a doctor inspired Dhruv to stay focused and disciplined.

After conversation Dhruv and Sarah was walking towards Main gate ,Insihka walked back of them , Dhruv was surprised after seeing Inshika in the college.

"Hey ,Inishka how are you , how come you are here , Dhruv asked ....Hold on ! Hold on ! Sarah shouted with surprise and asked Do you guys know each other ?

"Yes ! Of course We know each other from our school days Inishka replied to Sarah.

Inishka became one among them , The group quickly became inseparable, supporting each other through the highs and lows of college life.

They spent countless hours studying together, attending campus events, and exploring the city. Their diverse backgrounds and interests enriched Dhruv's college experience, exposing him to new perspectives and ideas. Their bond became stronger day by day .

A Quiet evening after a particularly challenging week , the group decided to have a quiet night in .

They gathered at Aarav's house. Enjoying a simple dinner and relaxed conversation .

As the night wore on the conversation turned reflective , with each other friend sharing personal stories and struggles.

Dhruv had always been reserved about his past , but surrounded by his closest friends , he felt a surge of trust and decided it was time to share his story.

Taking a deep breath, Dhruv began. "There's something I've been wanting to share with you all. It's a big part of who I am and why I'm so driven."His friends listened intently as Dhruv recounted his early childhood.

He spoke about his loving parents, who tragically passed away when he was very young, leaving him an orphan.

He described the heart-wrenching loss and the profound impact it had on his life."I was so young, and I didn't fully understand what had happened," Dhruv said, his voice wavering slightly.

"All I knew was that my world had been turned upside down."He then spoke about his grandmother, who took him in and raised him with immense love and care despite their difficult circumstances.

He described her strength, the sacrifices she made, and the wisdom she imparted."She was everything to me," Dhruv continued.

"She worked tirelessly to provide for us, even walking six kilometers each day for agricultural work. Despite her struggles, she always encouraged me to be strong and never give up."

Dhruv's voice grew heavier as he recounted the day his grandmother passed away. "Losing her was the hardest thing I've ever gone through. I felt completely alone.

As Dhruv shared his story, his friends listened in stunned silence, their hearts breaking for him.
Inishka, sitting closest to him, reached out and held his hand, tears glistening in her eyes."I know you very well about you Dhruv, But I didn't disturb you and never asked you about this in the school " she said softly.

"You're so incredibly strong."Aarav, Viraj, Rishi, and Sarah were equally moved. Each of them felt a deep sense of empathy and admiration for Dhruv, realizing the immense challenges he had overcome.

Dhruv continued, explaining how his grandmother's words and the memories of his parents had kept him going.

"Her encouragement and the memories of my parents pushed me to keep striving for a better future.
Every success I achieve is in honor of them."

The room was filled with a profound sense of connection and understanding. By sharing his story, Dhruv had allowed his friends to see a vulnerable side of him, deepening their bond even further.

His friends took turns expressing their support and admiration. "Dhruv, your resilience is inspiring," Viraj said, his voice filled with respect.

"Thank you for trusting us with your story.""We're here for you, always," Aarav added. "You're not alone anymore. We're your family too."Sarah nodded, wiping away tears.

"You've been through so much, and yet you've accomplished so much. We're so proud of you." And everyone hugged him and gave him a love and Trust.

Aarav's Mother Mrs. Laura overheard his story and come closer and told

"Dhruv , you're like a son to me now."

Placing a comforting hand on his shoulder. "Always remember , no matter how tough life gets ,you have a mother here and a family like friends.

Her words touched Dhruv deeply. Inishka squeezed Dhruv's hand, her eyes filled with love.

"You're one of the strongest person I know. Your past doesn't define you; it's shaped you into the incredible person you are today" . Inishka Replied!!

Sharing his story brought Dhruv a sense of relief and comfort.

He felt an even deeper connection to his friends, knowing they truly understood him now. In the days that followed, the friends were more supportive and attentive than ever.

They rallied around Dhruv, ensuring he knew he was loved and valued.

As the days went by, Mrs. Laura's home became a second home for Tommy.

He spent many weekends there, enjoying the warmth and Mother's love that filled the house. She treated him with the same care and affection she showed her own children, making him feel truly part of the family.

One day, as they sat in the garden, Mrs. Laura turned to Dhruv. "You know, Dhruv, love and family are not just about blood. It's about the bonds we create and the love we share.

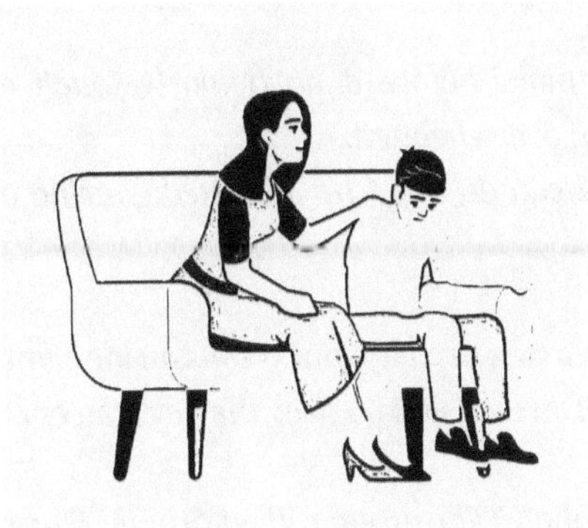

And the Dhruv's friends arrived at the scene and started conversations and had a much laughter .

Dhruv'sopenness inspired his friends to share more of their own stories and struggles, creating an environment of mutual trust and understanding.

Their bond grew unbreakable, built on a foundation of shared experiences, support, and genuine care for one another.

With a renewed sense of purpose and the unwavering support of his friends, Dhruv felt more determined than ever to honor his parents and grandmother's legacy.

He continued to pursue his dreams, knowing he had a family of friends who believed in him and stood by his side.

As the semester progressed, the coursework became increasingly demanding. Dhruv and his friends often found themselves in the library, working on assignments and preparing for exams.

Whenever one of them struggled, the others were quick to offer help *and encouragement.*

One memorable night before a particularly tough economics exam, Dhruv was feeling overwhelmed.
"I don't know if I can do this," he admitted, staring at his textbook in frustration.

Aarav, sensing Dhruv's anxiety, put a reassuring hand on his shoulder. "You've got this, Dhruv. Let's go over the key concepts together.

We'll make it through."The group rallied around Dhruv, breaking down the material and quizzing each other until they all felt confident.

During his junior year of college, Dhruv's fascination with robotics naturally extended to a growing interest in automobile design.

The idea of integrating advanced technology into vehicles to create smarter, safer, and more efficient transportation solutions captured his imagination. This new passion prompted him to delve into the world of automotive engineering.

Discovery of Passion

Dhruv's interest was piqued during a guest lecture by a renowned automotive designer, Ms. Karen Hayes, who spoke about the future of autonomous vehicles and the integration of AI in automotive systems.

Inspired by her vision, Dhruv began researching more about the field.

"I've always loved technology and innovation," Dhruv shared with Viraj about his love towards the passion.

"And now, seeing how it can transform the automotive industry is incredible.

I think I want to explore this further."Dhruv said to Viraj" .Viraj told about the Automotive club .

Dhruv joined the university's automotive club, where he met other students passionate about car design and engineering.

Among them were Chris, an engineering student specializing in aerodynamics, a design student with a flair for aesthetics.The club participated in various competitions, including designing and building prototypes for electric and autonomous vehicles.

These projects provided Dhruv with hands-on experience and allowed him to apply his knowledge of robotics in a new context.

And comes the Collaborative Projects ,One of the club's major projects was to design a prototype for an autonomous electric car. Dhruv wanted a team he went near his friends and told about the project they supported him , Dhruv teamed up with Aarav and Rishi to work on this ambitious project and other friends were looking after all their needs .

Aarav focused on optimizing the vehicle's aerodynamics, Rishi worked on the interior and exterior design, and Dhruv integrated the robotic and AI systems. They spent countless hours in the lab, testing and refining their prototype.

They faced numerous challenges, from ensuring the car's sensors worked accurately to designing a user-friendly interface.

Despite the hurdles, they made significant progress, driven by their shared passion and determination. For Dhruv it was a very important project as he was the main role in it .

Chris his opposite team person saw the work of Dhruv and thought he will win the project and he will receive all the needs and help from the mentors , Chris behaved selfish and one evening he moved to Dhruv's friend circle where everyone was sitting in the auditorium busy with their own stuff and Dhruv was in lab working on the Project .

Chris Walked towards them and started conversation about the campus and other things . And he started talking about Dhruv like , " That poor orphan fellow Dhruv , He is not a good person and he don't know the value of people and he make use of you all .

See , you guys are helping him in Project but he is getting highlighted in front of everyone , Dhruv friends became very furious and started " Hello , Excuse me Mind your own business , don't interfere and try to break our bond . "Why are you doing this ? Trying to tear us apart with lies only shows your own insecurities .

We won't be manipulated by anyone's words, we know better him than anyone .

And know one thing we are not that kind of friends who pray for his bad and feel Jealous of his works .

" True friends lift each other up . there's enough success for everyone and being supportive group makes the journey more fulfilling , We are the friends who always be in all his happiness and sadness , we never wish a negative vibes , we stand by his side through all of his life ,it may be ups and downs.
Now , "Don't over think about us and waste your time , We know how to hold our bonds stronger , you better get out of here." Dhruv friends Replied!!

Dhruv saw all these scenes , when they met in Mrs. Laura home for dinner Dhruv expressed his gratitude. "I can't thank you all enough for standing by me .

your support means world to me." His friends told Hey , charming boy don't worry and feel sad for anything , we are here for you always .

Aarav's mother Mrs. Laura felt very emotional and happy after seeing all them together with strong thoughts.

Dhruv after his lunch sat near steps , took out his Family photo and started telling about his friends and Mrs. Laura , I got a great friends moreover we became a family . They mean to me everything now ... Hmmmm I miss you people .... Tears dropped down on the frame and Dhruv felt depressed

And became stronger by himself and felt happy that he got all the love which he has been waiting for all these years and loneliness of years turned up with happier life .

As the days moved Recognizing Dhruv's potential, Dr. Patel, his robotics mentor, introduced him to Dr. Evans, a professor in the automotive engineering department.

Dr. Evans had extensive experience in automobile design and agreed to mentor Dhruv, providing invaluable guidance and insights.

"Dhruv, your background in robotics gives you a unique perspective," Dr. Evans said during one of their meetings. "Combining that with automotive engineering could lead to groundbreaking innovations.

Let's explore how we can push the boundaries of what's possible." And Dhruv project got success .

And everyone were impressed on his First small success , hard work and he celebrated his success with his friends in his Favorite place ; Aarav's home .

And then the days passed ,he got the Internship Opportunity .

In the summer before his senior year, Dhruv secured an internship at an innovative automotive company, AutoTech Innovations.

The company was known for its cutting-edge work in electric and autonomous vehicles.

This internship was a dream come true, offering Dhruv the chance to work on real-world projects and learn from industry experts.

At AutoTech Innovations, Dhruv was assigned to a team developing an advanced driver-assistance system (ADAS) for their latest electric vehicle.

His role involved integrating AI algorithms and sensor technologies to enhance the vehicle's safety and autonomous capabilities.

The internship provided Dhruv with hands-on experience and a deeper understanding of the automotive industry. It also reinforced his desire to combine his robotics expertise with automobile design to create smarter, more efficient vehicles.

His hard work never failed and he got one more opportunity of "Senior Year Capstone Project" , For his senior year capstone project, Dhruv decided to focus on designing an autonomous electric vehicle tailored for urban environments.

He envisioned a compact, efficient car that could navigate crowded city streets with ease.

Dhruv's friends rallied around him, offering their expertise and support.

Viraj helped with the software development, integrating advanced AI algorithms for autonomous navigation.

Aarav optimized the vehicle's aerodynamics, ensuring it was both efficient and stylish. Rishi worked on the design, creating a sleek, modern look that would appeal to urban drivers.

The project consumed countless hours, but the results were worth it.

Their autonomous electric vehicle prototype, named "CitySmart," impressed not only the faculty but also industry representatives who attended the final presentation.

Dhruv's work garnered praise for its innovation and practical application, earning him several job offers and the possibility of further developing CitySmart commercially.

One evening, as they gathered at Aarav's home as usual their favorite place, Dhruv shared his vision.

"I want to create a car that's not just efficient but also accessible to everyone, especially those in rural areas," he said !!

His eyes shining with enthusiasm.His friends listened intently, nodding in agreement.

After listening to his dream Mrs . Laura stepped forward to help him financially but Dhruv rejected it and everyone were shock and told him " Hey, Dhruv , take the amount it is very needed to you , "Dhruv replied I need to do this on my won . This project is my vision , and finding a way to make it work independently is part of the journey for me ."

His friends looked at him , concern and understanding in their eyes .

Aarav spoke gently , "Are you sure , Dhruv ? we just want to help ."
Dhruv nodded , his resolve unwavering .
"I'm sure . I want to prove to myself that I can overcome these challenges , It's not just about the money ; it's about the growth and lessons I"ll learn along the way .

" I need to find my own path ." If I need amount for the project I can manage through my savings which I did it from my childhood , that hard work money will pay off my dream car project .

I will be the most satisfied and happiest person if it get successes by that way And That project will be very special to me .

Mrs. Laura felt very happy and told I'm very proud of you . By the way who taught you the lesson of saving money Mrs. Laura asked ,
Dhruv Replied " I learnt it from my Granmda , Once she told me that
"Start saving a single coin , one or other day when you really want to use that it will turn into large amount and make you win" .

Don't waste it for small things , If you're saving , you're succeeding .
Saving Money should be a Priority"
These lines inspired me a lot but still Mrs. Laura I was stuck between I need to save money " and You only live once " thought of taking it and spending it to enjoy my life , but I couldn't do that because I always listen to Heart not on Mind .

Mrs. Laura and His friends was very Proud of him , his responsibilities and calculations of life inspired them . And His friend Inishka hugged him tightly .

After watching her love towards Dhruv ,their friends asked her that !

Do you like Dhruv ? " Inishka cheeks turned pink and she started expressing all the moments of her , Yes , I like him from the school days.

infact I joined this college because of Dhruv ...But I never expressed my feelings towards him ... I wanted him to spend all of his time on his carrier and get success , has he faced very hardships .

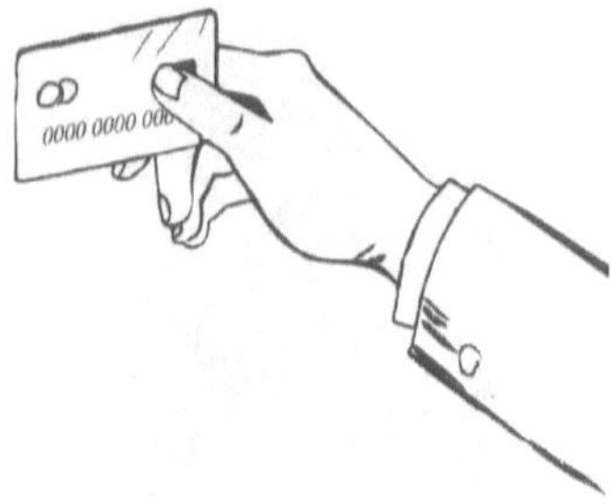

I was far away from him during school days , I observed every moment of his happiness and sadness during his days and I felt it from away , I wish I would have been with him when he was alone , but I wanted him to become stronger by himself !!! As I keep on telling there are soo many memories and moments to share ....

Let's help him for now and will see rest of the things what will happen."
Inishka Smiled and replied "
Dhruv went to the bank to get his Savings amount and Started to work on the Project .
Designing the Prototype:Dhruv began working on the prototype, spending countless hours in the college workshop.

He focused on integrating advanced robotics with practical design, aiming for a car that was both technologically advanced and affordable.

His friends often joined him, offering ideas and assistance. Viraj, with his tech expertise, helped Dhruv develop the software, while Rishi and Aarav contributed to the design and engineering aspects.
Sarah, with her organizational skills, kept track of their progress and deadlines.

Facing Challenges: Despite their combined efforts, the project faced numerous challenges.
Technical glitches, funding issues, and unforeseen setbacks tested their resolve. One night, after a particularly frustrating day, Dhruv sat in the workshop, his head in his hands.

"Maybe this is too ambitious," he muttered. "What if we can't make it work?" Inishka placed a reassuring hand on his shoulder.

"Dhruv, remember why you started this. Every great invention faces hurdles. We're here to support you, no matter what." This is not your end he have still more to go and Hard work will always pay off . Just believe in this .

Dhruv persevered. Gradually, they began to see progress. The prototype took shape, and the software started functioning smoothly.

Each small victory fueled their determination to keep going. Mrs. Laura often visited the workshop, bringing homemade meals and words of encouragement.

"You're doing something incredible" , Dhruv. Keep believing in yourself Mrs Laura was Motivating him .

"The Final Stretch: As they neared the completion of the prototype, Dhruv and his team faced one final challenge ,a critical component malfunctioned, threatening to delay the project significantly.

With limited funds and time, they had to find a solution quickly.

Virraj suggested reaching out to a local manufacturer for help.

"They might be able to provide the part we need at a lower cost."

Dhruv agreed, and they managed to secure the component, thanks to the manufacturer's support. The final assembly was tense, with everyone working late into the night to ensure everything was perfect. The day of the unveiling arrived, and excitement filled the air. Dhruv's friends, professors, and Mrs. Laura gathered to witness the culmination of their hard work.

Dhruv stood by the car, a sleek, innovative design that combined efficiency, accessibility, and advanced robotics."

Ladies and gentlemen," Dhruv began, his voice filled with emotion, "I present to you our new car, designed to bring advanced technology to everyone, regardless of their circumstances.

"The audience erupted in applause as Dhruv demonstrated the car's *features, showcasing its user-friendly interface, energy efficiency, and adaptability to various terrains.*

As the crowd admired the car, Dhruv's friends gathered around him, beaming with pride.

Inishka gave a hug and told. "You did it, Dhruv".

We all did it."Mrs. Laura's eyes glistened with tears. "

Your grandmother would be so proud of you, Dhruv.

You've created something truly remarkable. And the authorities appreciated him for the Great Work .

CHAPTER FIVE

The sun was setting , casting a golden hue across the meadow . This air was filled with sweet scent of cherry blossoms , their delicate petals dancing in thr gentle breeze . Dhruv had planned every detail , hoping to create a moment that Inishka would never forget and wanted to make that moment most memorable. As they Sat down near the old ancient oak tree " I have something for you , " Dhruv said , his voice steady but he hands slightly trembling .Dhruv got down on one knee , pulling out a simple but elegant ring .

The wind rustled the blossoms around them , sending a shower of petals into the air , creating a magical atmosphere .

Dhruv expressed all his love towards Inishka and told her " I know how much you love me , I heard everything that day when you were telling to our friends , wait for me until I get success in my life , Dhruv said it very emotionally!!

" Inishka accepted and replied Don't worry Dhruv I'm Here for you . As they embraced , the wind carried their laughter and emotional talks . and then blossoms seemed to dance in celebration .

Under the Oak tree , surrounded by the beauty of nature , Dhruv and Inishka promised to spend their lives together , creating a new chapter of their love .

”Moving Forward:The success of the prototype attracted attention from investors and industry experts, opening doors for further development and production.

Dhruv and his friends continued to work together, refining the design and exploring new innovations.
Their bond grew stronger, fueled by their shared achievements and the challenges they had overcome.

Dhruv's invention was not just a technological breakthrough but a testament to the power of perseverance, teamwork, and the support of true friends.

As Dhruv looked back on his journey, he realized that the car was more than just a product.

It was a symbol of resilience, friendship, and the unyielding spirit of innovation.

At a special event celebrating the car's widespread success, Dhruv raised a toast.

"To my friends and family, who believed in me and supported me every step of the way.

This car is our collective achievement, and it stands as a testament to what we can accomplish together."
Their glasses clinked, and the room filled with applause and laughter.

Dhruv knew that their journey was far from over. With the support of his friends and the inspiration of his past, he was ready to continue pushing the

boundaries of innovation, creating a legacy that would inspire future generations.

He started up with small company and turned up big achievement to him .
Despite their busy schedules.

Dhruv and Inishka made it a priority to find balance and spend quality time together.

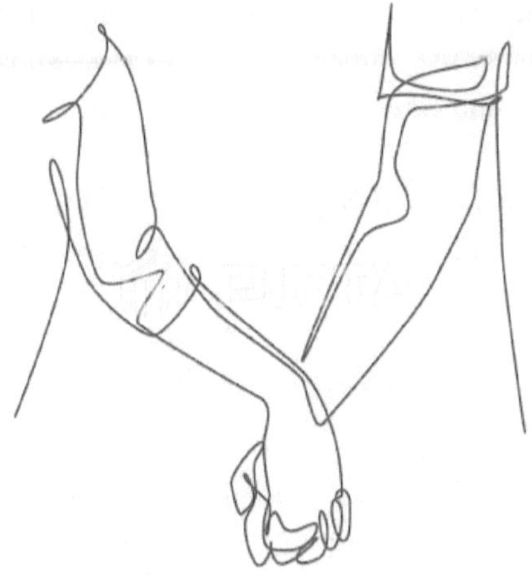

They understood the importance of nurturing their relationship and creating a life that was not just about work, but also about shared experiences and happiness.

They often took time to travel, explore new places, and enjoy the simple pleasures of life. Whether it was a quiet evening at home, a spontaneous weekend getaway, or attending community events, they cherished their moments together.

With the success of his car company, 'Dhruv's reputation as a visionary entrepreneur grew.

He saw opportunities in various industries and decided to expand his horizons.

Sitting ,one evening, he shared his ambitious plans to Inishka that

"I want to create companies that not only succeed but also make a positive impact on the world. We've done it with the car company; now let's take it further," Dhruv said.

His eyes gleaming with determination.Dhruv and his team embarked on an ambitious journey, launching ventures in technology, healthcare, renewable energy, and education.

Each company was founded on principles of innovation, sustainability, and social responsibility.

Dhruv and Inishka shared values and goals strengthened their bond.

They both believed in the power of kindness, the importance of giving back, and the value of hard work.
Their philanthropic efforts, which included funding educational programs, healthcare initiatives, and environmental projects, were a testament to their commitment to making a positive impact.

They often discussed their future plans and dreams, whether it was expanding their philanthropic work, exploring new business ventures, or simply enjoying their life together. Their ability to communicate openly and support each other's ambitions was a cornerstone of their happy life.

Dhruv founded a technology company focusing on artificial intelligence, cybersecurity, and software solutions.

The company quickly became a leader in the tech industry, known for its cutting-edge products and ethical practices.

Recognizing the importance of accessible healthcare, Dhruv started a healthcare company that developed affordable medical technologies and telemedicine solutions.

The company's innovations improved healthcare access for millions, particularly in underserved regions.
Passionate about environmental sustainability, Dhruv launched a renewable energy company specializing in solar and wind energy solutions.

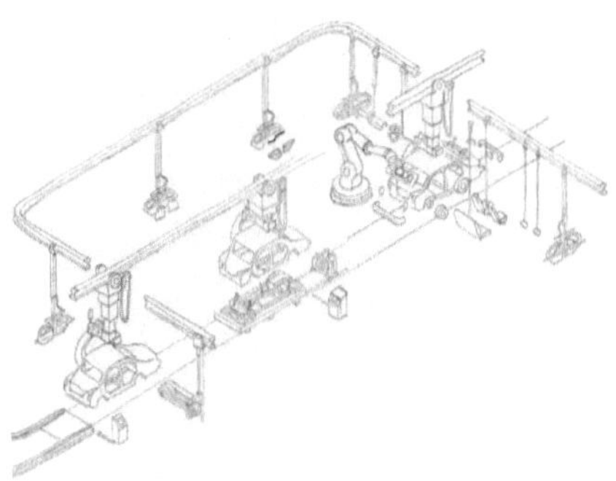

The company's projects significantly reduced carbon footprints and promoted clean energy adoption worldwide.

Dhruv'scommitment to education led to the creation of an educational technology company that provided digital learning tools and resources.

The company's initiatives helped bridge educational gaps and empower students globally.

CHAPTER SIX

Building an Empire

As these companies thrived, Dhruv's business empire expanded rapidly. His leadership style, characterized by ethical decision-making, innovation, and a focus on social impact, attracted top talent and investors.

The companies' success was a testament to Dhruv's visionary approach and commitment to excellence.
Despite his growing wealth, Dhruv remained grounded and focused on giving back.

He established the Foundation, which funded numerous social initiatives, including scholarships, healthcare programs, and environmental conservation projects.

Dhruv's philanthropic efforts extended beyond financial contributions. He actively participated in community projects, mentored young entrepreneurs, and advocated for policies that promoted social equity and environmental sustainability.

Building and managing multiple successful companies came with its share of challenges.

Market fluctuations, regulatory hurdles, and intense competition tested Dhruv'sresilience.

However, his integrity and commitment to his values guided him through these challenges.

During a particularly challenging economic downturn, Dhruv's companies faced significant financial pressures.

Rather than resorting to layoffs, Dhruv implemented creative cost-saving measures and focused on innovation to navigate the crisis.

His compassionate leadership earned him immense respect and loyalty from his employees.

Dhruv'sbusiness acumen and ethical approach led to unprecedented success.

His companies continued to grow, diversify, and innovate, solidifying his status as the richest person in the world. However, wealth was never his primary motivation; it was a byproduct of his relentless pursuit of excellence and positive impact.

At a grand event celebrating his achievements,
Dhruv addressed a crowd of industry leaders, employees, and supporters.

"Our success is not just about financial gain. It's about creating value, *driving innovation, and making a meaningful difference in the world."*

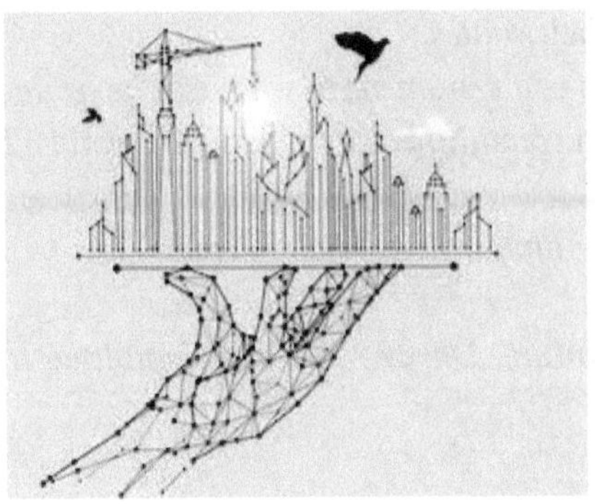

Dhruv's journey to becoming the richest person in the world was characterized by integrity, vision, and a deep sense of responsibility.

His story inspired countless individuals to pursue their dreams while staying true to their values.
"Dhruv's success is a testament to what can be achieved with passion, dedication, and a commitment to making the world a better place.

We've built something truly special together.

Looking to the future, Dhruv remained committed to innovation and social impact.

He explored new opportunities in emerging technologies, sustainable practices, and global development.
His vision continued to inspire his team and the wider business community.

Dhruv's companies set new standards for corporate responsibility, demonstrating that success and integrity could go hand in hand.

His leadership style, focused on empathy, collaboration, and ethical decision-making, became a model for future generations of entrepreneurs.

Years later, Dhruv legacy as a visionary entrepreneur and philanthropist endured.

At a special ceremony, he received a lifetime achievement award for his contributions to business, technology, and society.

Addressing the audience, Dhruv's shared his reflections."This journey has been about more than just building companies. It's been about creating a positive impact and showing that success is measured not just by wealth, but by the difference we make in the lives of others."

The audience, filled with people whose lives had been touched by Dhruv'swork, applauded warmly.
His friends, who had been his steadfast allies throughout his journey, stood by him with pride and admiration. Together, they celebrated a life dedicated to innovation, integrity, and compassion.
Dhruv'sstory remained a powerful testament to the transformative power of vision and the enduring impact of leading with heart and purpose.

This chapter highlights Dhruv's **TRIUMPH Means BIG VICTORY,** *journey to becoming the richest person , focusing on his entrepreneurial ventures, innovative vision, and commitment to social impact.*
It underscores the values that guided him and the legacy he built through his diverse and successful business endeavors.

After achieving significant success with his car invention and establishing a promising career and Many companies ,
Dhruv's kind-hearted nature wanted him to start Orphan age home

which should be Most safest and should be filled with lots of love and desire to give back to society led him to start it His intention was to shower a love on Orphan people . These ashrams became sanctuaries for those in need, reflecting David's enduring compassion and commitment to making a difference.

This chapter chronicles his journey from a successful inventor to a philanthropist dedicated to serving the less fortunate.

This chapter chronicles his journey from a successful inventor to a philanthropist dedicated to serving the less fortunate.

Dhruv's life took a meaningful turn as he reflected on his journey and the challenges he had overcome.

His experiences of loss, struggle, and resilience had shaped him into a compassionate individual who wanted to help others find hope and stability. Dhruv began working on his first ashram.

He chose a serene location near his hometown, envisioning a place that would provide not just physical shelter but also emotional and spiritual support.planning and construction started .

Dhruv started managing the ashram's resources and donations, Inishka with her background in psychology, planned programs for emotional and mental well-being.

The ashram soon opened its doors, welcoming people from all walks of life—orphans, the elderly, and those who had faced significant hardships.

The Midland Orphange: drawn from memory by Reg Meakin.
In the foreground the Leen flows past the end of Friar Street.
Drawing carried out in 1983.

Dhruv ensured that the ashram offered a range of services, including educational programs, vocational training, and counseling sessions.

Dhruv spent a lot of time at the ashram, interacting with the residents, listening to their stories, and offering words of encouragement.

His kindness and genuine care touched the hearts of many, creating a warm and supportive community.

Encouraged by the success of the first ashram, Dhruv decided to expand his mission.

With the donations from well-wishers, he established more ashrams in different regions, each tailored to the specific needs of the local community.

Each ashram became a beacon of hope, providing education, healthcare, and a safe haven for those in need. Dhruv's reputation as a compassionate leader grew, and more people came forward to support his mission.

Running the ashrams was not without challenges.

Funding, staffing, and managing the needs of the residents required constant effort and dedication.

His friends remained by his side, helping him navigate these challenges with their expertise and unwavering support.

One particularly challenging period saw a severe shortage of funds. Dhruv considered scaling back operations but his friends rallied together to organize a fundraiser, bringing the community together to support the cause.

As the years passed, Dhruv's ashrams became well-established, helping thousands of people rebuild their lives. His kind-hearted nature and dedication to making a difference had created a lasting impact on countless lives.

At a celebration marking the tenth anniversary of the first ashram, Dhruvaddressed the crowd. "This journey has been about more than just providing shelter. It's about creating a family, offering hope, and showing kindness.

I am grateful to everyone who has supported this mission.

"His friends, standing beside him, echoed his sentiments.

Inishka, now his wife, spoke about the emotional and psychological support provided by the ashrams.
"We've seen people transform, find their strength, and rebuild their lives. Dhruv's vision has given us all a purpose and a way to give back."

Mrs .Laura , who had always been a guiding figure in Dhruv'slife, attended the celebration. She hugged Dhruv warmly, her eyes filled with pride. Dhruv. You've turned your kindness into a powerful force for good.

Looking ahead, Dhruv continued to innovate, finding new ways to support and uplift those in need.
He collaborated with educational institutions, healthcare providers, and social workers to expand the services offered at the ashrams.

His story became an inspiration, encouraging others to take action and support those less fortunate.

His story became an inspiration, encouraging others to take action and support those less fortunate.

Dhruv's ashrams stood as a testament to the enduring power of kindness and the profound impact one individual can make.

Dhruv's ashrams continued to thrive, a living legacy of his compassion and dedication.

At a grand celebration, surrounded by friends, family, and the many lives he had touched, Dhruv reflected on his journey.

"Starting these ashrams was one of the most fulfilling decisions of my life. It's a reminder that no matter where we come from or what we've faced, we have the power to make a difference.

Kindness, compassion, and a desire to help others can create ripples of change."

The audience, filled with people who had been touched by Dhruv'swork, applauded warmly.

His friends, who had been with him through every step of the journey, looked at him with pride and admiration.

Together, they raised a toast to Dhruv's unwavering kindness and the lasting legacy he had built. The ashrams, born from a kind heart and a desire to give back, stood as enduring symbols of hope, compassion, and the power of community.

The interview was held in a grand auditorium filled with eager young minds, aspiring entrepreneurs, and business leaders. The atmosphere was electric with anticipation as Dhruv took the stage, greeted by enthusiastic applause. The interviewer, a well-respected journalist, welcomed him warmly.

" Mr. Dhruv, you've had an extraordinary journey. As you reflect on your path, who are the people you are most grateful for?"

Dhruv smiled, thinking about the friends who had stood by him through thick and thin.

"I owe a great deal to my friends who have been my pillars of support and strength. Viraj, Aarav,Rishi , Sarah and Aarav mother Mrs. Laura who cared me like her son and others have been there since the beginning, offering their unwavering support, encouragement, and companionship.

Their loyalty and belief in me have been invaluable."He continued, "There were times when the journey was incredibly tough, and their presence made all the difference.

They celebrated my successes and stood by me during failures. Our bond has always been based on trust, respect, and a shared vision for making a positive impact.

Mr. Dhruv, thank you for joining us today. Your journey has been nothing short of extraordinary, and many here are eager to learn from your experiences.

" Mr. Dhruv, you've had an extraordinary journey. As you reflect on your path, who are the people you are most grateful for?"

Dhruv smiled, thinking about the friends who had stood by him through thick and thin.

"I owe a great deal to my friends who have been my pillars of support and strength. Viraj, Aarav,Rishi , Sarah and Aarav mother Mrs. Laura who cared me like her son and others have been there since the beginning, offering their unwavering support, encouragement, and companionship.

Their loyalty and belief in me have been invaluable."He continued, "There were times when the journey was incredibly tough, and their presence made all the difference.

They celebrated my successes and stood by me during failures. Our bond has always been based on trust, respect, and a shared vision for making a positive impact.

"Turning his attention to Inishka, who was seated in the audience, Dhruv's eyes filled with love and admiration. "Inishka, my incredible wife, has been my rock. Her support, wisdom, and love have been the foundation of our shared success.

She has been by my side through every challenge, offering her insights and keeping me grounded."Dhruv paused, his voice full of emotion. "Inishka's compassion and dedication to our philanthropic

efforts have been inspiring.

She has played a crucial role in managing our initiatives and ensuring that we stay true to our values. I am deeply grateful for her partnership, both in business and in life.

By Remembering His Grandmother Dhruv'sexpression softened as he spoke about his grandmother, the woman who had shaped his early years and instilled in him the values that guided his life.

"My grandmother, who raised me after my parents passed away, was a beacon of strength and wisdom. She taught me the importance of hard work, integrity, and kindness."

He continued, "Even when we faced financial hardships, she never lost hope and always encouraged me to pursue my dreams.

Let's start by asking, what motivated you to pursue such diverse ventures and ultimately become a leading figure in multiple industries?"Dhruv smiled, taking a moment to reflect before answering.

"My motivation has always been a combination of curiosity, a desire to solve problems, and a commitment to making a positive impact.

Each venture I pursued stemmed from a passion for innovation and a belief that business can be a force for good.

"He continued, "For example, my car company was born from a passion for automobiles and a vision to create sustainable transportation solutions.

My healthcare and educational ventures were driven by a desire to improve access and quality for all.
It's important to stay true to your passions and let them guide your entrepreneurial journey."The interviewer leaned forward.

The interviewer asked about the challenges Dhruv faced along the way. "You've encountered numerous obstacles.

How did you manage to overcome them and keep moving forward?"

Dhruv nodded thoughtfully. "Challenges are inevitable, but they are also opportunities for growth.

Perseverance is key.

There were times when things seemed insurmountable, but I always focused on the bigger picture and stayed committed to my goals. "Surround yourself with a supportive team, be adaptable, and never lose sight of your vision."

The interviewer turned to the audience.

Be compassionate, give back to your community, and lead with empathy. Your actions can inspire others and create a ripple effect of positive change."

"What advice would you give to the young aspiring entrepreneurs here today?"

Dhruv'seyes scanned the eager faces in the audience.

"First and foremost, believe in yourself and your vision.

Take calculated risks and be prepared to learn from failure.

Innovation often comes from experimentation and learning from what doesn't work.

Build a strong network, seek mentors, and be open to feedback."He paused, letting the message sink in. "Also, remember that success is not just about financial gain. It's about creating value, making a positive impact, and staying true to your values.

Your potential is limitless, and you have the power to create a better future for yourselves and for others. Stop thinking that "I can't do that it's very hard etc etc
First set your mind and aim that let me see who is stronger and take a step forward , you will be the success person whatever the matter or thing is !!!

And stop thinking that I will do it tomorrow , Do today what should be done , your tomorrow never come, and you can't predict what will happen tomorrow. The audience erupted in applause, deeply moved by Dhruv's words.

As he left the stage, many felt inspired and motivated to pursue their dreams with the same passion and integrity that had guided Dhruv on his remarkable journey.

CHAPTER SEVEN

A Strong Partnership

Dhruv and Inishka's relationship had always been built on a foundation of mutual respect, shared values, and a deep understanding of each other's dreams and aspirations.

As Dhruv's ventures flourished, Inishka stood by his side, offering unwavering support and contributing her own skills and insights to their shared endeavors.

Dhruv and Inishka created a warm and welcoming home, filled with love, laughter,Their home was a place where friends and family were always welcome, and where they could retreat from the world and enjoy their time together.

Their Friends used to come to their home and they used to the same Crazy things which they used to do in college .

Inishka's passion for gardening transformed their backyard into a beautiful oasis, where they often spent time relaxing and connecting *with nature.*

Dhruv, Inishka , and their friends decided to take a much-needed break from their busy lives and embark on a memorable road trip. This chapter captures the joy, adventures, and bonding moments they experienced together, creating memories that would last a lifetime.

It was a bright and sunny morning when Dhruv, Inishka, Viraj, Aarav ,Rishi , Sarah gathered in Dhruv and Inishka's house, ready for their road trip.

Their destination was a beautiful coastal town, known for its serene beaches and picturesque landscapes.Inishka, with her infectious enthusiasm, had meticulously planned the trip.

She had mapped out the scenic routes, booked cozy accommodations, and prepared a playlist of everyone's favorite songs.

"Ready to hit the road?"Dhruv asked, his eyes sparkling with excitement."Absolutely!" everyone replied in unison, their faces beaming with anticipation.

As they set off, the atmosphere in the car was filled with laughter, music, and animated conversations. Viraj, who was a great storyteller, entertained everyone with his humorous anecdotes, while .

Dhruv and Inishka shared the driving responsibilities, allowing each of them to enjoy the stunning views and relax by fire camp .

The journey was punctuated with impromptu stops at quaint roadside cafes, scenic overlooks, and charming little towns.Bonding One of the highlights of the trip was a hike through a lush forest leading to a breathtaking waterfall.

The group navigated the trail with a mix of determination and playful banter. When they finally reached the waterfall, the sight was nothing short of magical. The cascading water, the mist in the air, and the surrounding greenery created a perfect backdrop for a group photo."Let's capture this moment," Inishka suggested, pulling out her camera.

They posed together, their smiles reflecting the happiness of the moment.

Later, they found a secluded spot by a river for a picnic. They spread out blankets, unpacked the delicious food they had brought, and enjoyed a leisurely meal. The sound of the flowing water and the chirping of birds added to the peaceful ambiance.

As the sun began to set, painting the sky with hues of orange and pink, the group gathered around a bonfire at their campsite. The crackling fire and the warmth of the flames created a cozy atmosphere, perfect for deeper conversations.Dhruv, reflecting on the day, said, "I'm so grateful for moments like these.

It's a reminder of how important it is to take a break and spend time with the people we care about."Inishka nodded in agreement. "This trip has been amazing. It's not just about the destination, but the journey and the experiences we share along the way."Rishi, poking the fire with a stick, added, "We should make this an annual tradition. These moments are what life is all about."

The trip was filled with unexpected surprises that added to the adventure. One day, they stumbled upon a local festival in a small town. The streets were lined with colorful stalls, music filled the air, and the aroma of delicious food wafted through the crowd.

The group immersed themselves in the festivities, trying local delicacies, dancing to the lively music, and even participating in a friendly tug-of-war competition.

Viraj, with his usual charm, managed to win a stuffed toy at a game booth and presented it to Inishka with a flourish. "For the best trip planner ever!" he declared, making everyone laugh.As the road trip came to an end, the group reflected on the memories they had created together.

They had shared laughter, faced challenges, and strengthened their bonds. The trip was a reminder of the importance of friendship, love, and the joy of shared experiences.

On the last night, as they gathered around the bonfire once more, Dhruv raised a toast. "To friendship, love, and unforgettable adventures.

Here's to many more trips and memories together."Everyone clinked their glasses, their hearts full of gratitude and happiness.

The road trip had not only given them a break from their routines but had also reinforced the value of their relationships and the importance of taking time to enjoy life's simple pleasures.

The Rise of Dhruv's Company Dhruv's car company, built on innovation and a passion for excellence, had grown rapidly.

His revolutionary designs and commitment to quality had earned him a stellar reputation in the automotive industry.

With success came expansion, and soon Dhruv's company was producing vehicles on a large scale.
However, during a routine quality check, one of the engineers discovered a significant flaw in the latest car model. The issue, a critical design flaw in the braking system, posed a serious safety risk.

It was a devastating blow to Dhruv , who had always prided himself on the safety and reliability of his vehicles.

Immediate Action Dhruv called an emergency meeting with his top engineers and managers.

"Our customers' safety is our top priority," he asserted firmly.

"We need to address this issue immediately, regardless of the cost."

The company halted production of the affected models and issued a recall for all units that had already been sold.

This decision, though financially costly, was necessary to uphold the company's commitment to safety and integrity.

Facing the Public Dhruv held a press conference to address the issue.

"We have discovered a flaw in one of our car models that could

compromise safety," he said candidly.

"We are taking immediate action to rectify this problem and ensure the safety of our customers.

I apologize for any inconvenience this may cause, and we are committed to making things right."Internal Investigation and Reorganization Dhruv launched a thorough internal investigation to understand how such a significant flaw had gone unnoticed. The investigation revealed that rapid expansion had led to lapses in the quality control processes.

To prevent such issues in the future, Dhruv implemented stricter quality control measures and reorganized the company's engineering and production departments.

Rallying the Team Dhruv's leadership was crucial during this crisis.

He worked closely with his team, motivating them to focus on solutions rather than dwelling on the setback. "We've faced challenges before, and we've overcome them," he reminded his staff.

"This is no different. We will learn from this and emerge stronger."

Inishka, always his confidante, helped him navigate the stress and pressure. "We've built this company on strong values," she reminded him.

"Staying true to those values will see us through this challenge."

Dhruv's friends, many of whom were now part of his business circle, also offered their support and assistance.

They stood by him, helping to manage the public relations crisis and ensuring that the recall process was smooth and efficient.

Rebuilding Trust The recall process was extensive, but Dhruv's transparency and dedication to resolving the issue earned him respect from customers and industry peers alike.

His company offered free repairs and replacements, and provided compensation for any inconvenience caused.

These actions, though costly, were necessary to rebuild trust with their customer base.

Determined to turn the crisis into an opportunity for improvement, Dhruv and his team worked tirelessly to redesign the flawed model.

They introduced new safety features and enhancements, making the updated version one of the safest and most advanced cars on the market.

When the new model was released, it received rave reviews for its innovative design and enhanced safety measures. The public appreciated the company's transparency and dedication to quality, and sales quickly rebounded.

Through this experience, Dhruv's company emerged stronger and more resilient.

The incident reinforced the importance of maintaining high standards and the willingness to take responsibility for mistakes.

Dhruv's handling of the crisis became a case study in business ethics and crisis management.

Dhruv's story, now marked by another significant challenge overcome, continued to inspire. His journey from a struggling orphan to a successful entrepreneur was a testament to the power of resilience, integrity, and unwavering commitment to one's values.

Dhruv and Inishka's Growing Family

As Dhruv and Inishka's love flourished, they welcomed a child into their lives.
Their son, Reyansh , was the joy of their hearts, growing up in a home filled with love and the values Dhruv and Inishka's cherished deeply.

Despite their busy lives, they made sure to spend quality time with Reyansh , teaching him the importance of hard work, kindness, and integrity.

However, as Reyansh grew older, Dhruv and Inishka noticed troubling signs of irresponsibility.

Unlike his father, Reyansh lacked a sense of discipline and commitment. He often neglected his studies, spent money recklessly, and showed little interest in the family business or any constructive activities.

Dhruv and Inishka's concerns grew as Reyansh 's behavior continued.

They tried talking to him, hoping to understand his perspective and guide him towards a more responsible path.

"Reyansh , you have so much potential," Dhruv would say. "But you need to apply yourself and take responsibility for your actions."

Reyansh's , however, often dismissed their concerns, believing that his parents' success meant he didn't need to worry about his future. "Why work so hard when everything is already taken care of?" he would retort.

The turning point came when Reyansh's reckless spending and poor decisions led to a serious incident.

He had borrowed a large sum of money to fund a lavish party, only to find himself unable to repay the debt.

The lenders began to harass him, and the situation quickly escalated.

Realizing the severity of the situation, Reyansh reluctantly turned to his parents for help.

Dhruv and Inishka were shocked but not entirely surprised. They saw this as an opportunity for a crucial lesson. And Dhruv told him that " My dear son , whatever may be the situation , Don't barrow money from anyone , Remember one thing your hand should always be for giving , not for taking. Build up such attitude . Dhruv told !!

Instead of simply bailing Reyansh out, Dhruv decided to take a tough love approach.

"We'll help you, Reyansh , but this is a chance for you to learn responsibility," he said firmly.

"You will work to repay this debt, and you will understand the value of hard work and accountability.

"Dhruv arranged for Reyansh to work at the family's car manufacturing plant, starting from the ground up.

Reyansh was tasked with various responsibilities, from manual labor to learning about the business operations. It was a drastic change from his previous lifestyle.

At first, Reyansh struggled with the new routine.

The work was demanding, and he often felt frustrated and overwhelmed. However, as time passed, he began to appreciate the effort and dedication required to build and maintain the business.

Through his work, Reyansh started to understand the values his parents had tried to instill in him.

He saw the respect his father earned from his employees, the pride in their craftsmanship, and the importance of integrity in every aspect of the business.

A Gradual Transformation
Slowly but surely, Reyansh's attitude began to change. He took pride in his work, started managing his finances more responsibly, and even showed interest in learning more about the business.

The experience humbled him and taught him the value of hard work and perseverance.

Rebuilding Trust Reyansh's transformation didn't happen overnight, but his parents noticed the positive changes. He became more responsible and respectful, and his relationship with Dhruv and Inishka improved significantly.

They were proud of his growth and the man he was becoming. One evening, after a long day at the plant, Reyansh sat down with Dhruv.

"Dad, I understand now," he said sincerely. "I see why you and Mom have always emphasized responsibility and hard work.

I'm sorry for not listening earlier, but I'm grateful for the lessons."

Dhruv smiled, placing a hand on his son's shoulder. "I'm proud of you, Reyansh . It's never too late to change and make a positive impact.

Remember, our legacy isn't just about success but about how we live our lives and treat others."

Looking Forward With a renewed sense of purpose, Reyansh became more involved in the family business, contributing fresh ideas and energy.

He embraced the values his parents had always cherished and aimed to uphold the legacy of integrity and hard work.

As Reyansh continued to grow and evolve within the family business, he discovered a passion for innovation.

Inspired by his father's journey and the principles he had learned, Reyansh was determined to make his mark and contribute to the company's legacy in a meaningful way.

The Breakthrough Idea One day, while working on a project at the company's research and development lab, Reyansh came up with a groundbreaking idea for a new type of eco-friendly vehicle.

Combining advanced technology with sustainable materials, Reyansh envisioned a car that not only reduced environmental impact but also set new standards for efficiency and performance.

He spent months refining his concept, working closely with engineers and designers.

Reyansh's enthusiasm and dedication were infectious, and he soon had a team of passionate individuals supporting his vision.

When Reyansh felt confident in his prototype, he presented his idea to the company's board of directors, including Dhruv.

The presentation was detailed and compelling, showcasing the potential of the new vehicle to revolutionize the automotive industry.

"By embracing sustainability and cutting-edge technology, we can lead the way in creating a greener future,"
Reyansh concluded, his eyes shining with determination. "This is not just a car; it's a statement about our commitment to innovation and responsibility."

Overcoming Skepticism While many were impressed by Reyansh's vision, there were also skeptics.
Some board members were concerned about the risks and costs associated with developing such an ambitious project.

However, Dhruv stood by his son, recognizing the same drive and passion that had fueled his own success.
"We've always been pioneers in this industry," Dhruv reminded the board. "Taking calculated risks and pushing the boundaries of what's possible is part of our legacy. I believe in Reyansh's vision and the potential it has to shape the future."

Greenlight and Development With Dhruv's support and a majority vote from the board, the project was greenlit.

Reyansh worked tirelessly, pouring their hearts and souls into

developing the new eco-friendly vehicle.
The process was challenging, with numerous setbacks and hurdles to overcome, but Reyansh's leadership and commitment never wavered.

The Grand Unveiling After years of hard work, the moment finally arrived. The new vehicle, named the "EcoVanguard," was ready for its grand unveiling.

The event was held at the company's headquarters, attended by industry leaders, environmental advocates, and media from around the world.

As Reyansh took the stage, he felt a mix of nerves and excitement. He glanced at his parents, who were sitting in the front row, their faces beaming with pride.

Taking a deep breath, he began his presentation.

"Today, we are not just launching a new car; we are introducing a new era of automotive innovation," Reyansh declared.

"The EcoVanguard represents our commitment to sustainability, performance, and the future of our planet. This is our legacy for the next generation.

"A Historic AchievementThe response to the EcoVanguard was overwhelmingly positive.

Industry experts praised its innovative design and environmental benefits, while customers were eager to embrace a vehicle that aligned with their values.

The EcoVanguard quickly became a best-seller, earning numerous awards and setting new standards in the industry.

Reyansh's achievement was celebrated as a milestone for the company and the automotive world.

He had not only proven his capabilities but had also honored the values his parents had instilled in him.

His success marked the beginning of a new chapter for the family business, one that was firmly rooted in innovation and responsibility.

Dhruv and Inishka were immensely proud of Reyansh . His journey from an irresponsible youth to a visionary leader was a testament to the power of perseverance, guidance, and personal growth.

Reyansh's achievement not only secured the future of the company but also reinforced the legacy of integrity and innovation that Tommy had worked so hard to build.

As Reyansh continued to grow and evolve within the family business, he discovered a passion for innovation.

Inspired by his father's journey and the principles he had learned, Alex was determined to make his mark and contribute to the company's legacy in a meaningful way.

One day, while working on a project at the company's research and development lab, Reyansh came up with a groundbreaking idea for a new type of eco-friendly vehicle.

Combining advanced technology with sustainable materials, Reyansh envisioned a car that not only reduced environmental impact but also set new standards for efficiency and performance.

He spent months refining his concept, working closely with engineers and designers. Reyansh's enthusiasm and dedication were infectious, and he soon had a team of passionate individuals supporting his vision.

When Reyansh felt confident in his prototype, he presented his idea to the company's board of directors, including Dhruv.

The presentation was detailed and compelling, showcasing the potential of the new vehicle to revolutionize the automotive industry.

Reyansh's achievement not only secured the future of the company but also reinforced the legacy of integrity and innovation that Tommy had worked so hard to build.

Reyansh in the Spotlight
As the EcoVanguard gained popularity, so did Reyansh. His innovative approach to sustainable automotive design caught the attention of major media outlets.

Soon, Reyansh found himself in the spotlight, featured in prominent magazines and news channels around the world.

The EcoVanguard Visionary Reyansh's first major feature came from Innovator's Monthly, a leading technology and business magazine.

The cover displayed a confident Alex standing beside the EcoVanguard, with the headline: "

Reyansh's Journey to Revolutionize the Automotive Industry.

"In the in-depth interview, Reyansh shared his journey from a reckless youth to a responsible leader, highlighting the support of his parents and the values they instilled in him.

"My father taught me that true success lies in creating a positive impact," he said.

"The EcoVanguard is a testament to our commitment to sustainability and innovation."

Following the magazine feature, Reyansh appeared on several popular television shows.

He discussed the EcoVanguard's development process, the challenges he faced, and the importance of sustainable innovation.

On one show, the host asked him about his motivations. "I wanted to create something that would not only succeed in the market but also contribute to a better world," Reyansh explained.

"We need to think about the future and how our actions today impact the generations to come."

Reyansh fame grew internationally. He was invited to speak at conferences and universities around the world, sharing his insights on sustainability and innovation.

His speeches were well-received, inspiring young entrepreneurs to pursue their dreams with purpose and integrity.

One notable event was the Global Innovation Summit, where Reyansh was the keynote speaker.

"Innovation is not just about technology," he told the audience. "It's about responsibility and creating solutions that benefit everyone, including our planet."

He spoke about his family's influence.

"My parents, especially my father, played a crucial role in my life," Reyansh said. "

Their support, guidance, and the values they instilled in me shaped who I am today. I owe my success to them."

Dhruv Perspective Watching his son's rise to fame, Dhruv felt immense *pride.*

He saw Reyansh's achievements as a continuation of their family legacy and a testament to the values he had worked hard to instill.

Dhruv often accompanied Reyansh to events, proudly watching his son inspire others.

During a joint interview, Dhruv expressed his thoughts.

"Seeing Reyansh achieve so much and stay true to our values is incredibly fulfilling," he said.
"It's not just about the success; it's about the impact we make and the legacy we leave behind."

As Reyansh 's public profile grew, he had to learn to balance his professional responsibilities with his personal life.

He made a conscious effort to spend quality time with his family, especially INISHKA , ever supportive, stood by Reyansh, helping him navigate the challenges of being in the public eye.

"Reyansh and Dhruv became a role model for many.

His story of transformation, innovation, and responsibility resonated with people across the globe.

He continued to push boundaries, always looking for new ways to innovate and make a positive impact
Reyansh's fame was not just about his achievements but also about the values he represented.

He was a living example of how perseverance, integrity, and a commitment to making the world a better place could lead to true success.

And one evening Dhruv sat with Inishka and told " I'm Very happy now, Reyansh made it, which I couldn't make out some things . He proved and showed What is the actual purpose of our lives.. He took me very up.

My life before was like Fish without water but now By all hard work , dedication I'm living a best life . The words I got stuck to , made me success today !! I was just small boy who was orphan and not known to anyone , but now I'm in many people hearts and in the Headlines "

....

SUCCESS
Sum of Efforts

*"**ROAD TO TRIUMPH**" Refers to the journey or path one takes to achieve success or victory. It suggests overcoming challenges, preserving through hardships, and ultimately reaching one's goals. Triumph is not just about the end result, but also the efforts, struggles, and personal growth experienced along the way with all ups and downs, Which is filled with Love, Hard work, Emotions, Loss of loved ones. Life turns good for some people and sometimes bad, We should try to make it something success.*

Purpose of our life is to Prove something, Everyone has their own capability and ability in one or other thing. Try to bring it out, Work hard and stick to the Words and aims, You will never Fail. Stop comparing you with others that will drag you down and lose confidence. Be yourself and Prove yourself.

Wishing well for others cultivates positivity and kindness. It will improve your own mental and Emotional well being while fostering supportive and compassionate environment around you. Being genuinely happy for other's successes and offering encouragement takes you very high in people's heart. Don't be jealous for others success, Someone else's success does not diminish your own potential or achievements Our life vary greatly from person to person, Prove that you are good at something and make it shine.

HARSHINI MAHESH